CRAFTY CHAMELEON

Books written by Mwenye Hadithi and illustrated by Adrienne Kennaway

Greedy Zebra
Hot Hippo
Crafty Chameleon
Tricky Tortoise
Lazy Lion
Baby Baboon

First paperback edition

First published in Great Britain in 1987 by
Hodder and Stoughton Children's Books,
a division of Hodder and Stoughton Ltd,
338 Euston Road, London NW1 3BH

Library of Congress Cataloging-in-Publication Data
Mwenye Hadithi
Crafty Chameleon.

Summary: A chameleon bedevilled by a leopard and a crocodile
uses his wits to get them to leave him alone.
(1. Chameleon - Fiction) I. Moore, Adrienne.
1945-   iii. II. Title
PZ7.M975Cr   1987   (E)   87-3867
ISBN 0 316 33723 4 (hc)
ISBN 0 316 33771 4 (pb)

10 9 8 7 6 5 4 3 2 1

Printed in Belgium

CRAFTY CHAMELEON

by **Mwenye Hadithi**

Illustrated by **Adrienne Kennaway**

Little, Brown and Company
Boston New York Toronto London

Every morning Chameleon rested and caught flies
in the high branches of the Mugumu tree.

Every morning Leopard came jumping and leaping from branch to branch, landing beside Chameleon with a heavy THUD!

And poor Chameleon bounced high into the air,
going around and around and around,
until he hit the ground with a SMACK!

One day Chameleon shouted angrily:

"If you don't leave me alone I shall tie you up with a rope — just like a dog!"

"Hah!" laughed the Leopard. And he bounced away.

Now, every evening Chameleon walked to the river
to drink with the other small animals.

And every evening, Crocodile came swishing and slithering out of the water, snakking his teeth and laughing as all the small animals ran away.

One day Chameleon shouted angrily:

"If you don't leave me alone I shall tie you up with a rope — just like a dog!"

"Hah hah hah!" laughed the Crocodile, shutting his teeth with a great big SNAKK!

So Chameleon asked the Weaving Birds to weave
him a rope of convolvulus vines, and he disguised
himself as a stone.

And when Leopard came bouncing along,
Chameleon threw the rope round his neck, calling:

"Now that I have you on a rope I shall pull you along!
Just wait until I pull."

Leopard waited, laughing, for he knew the tiny
Chameleon couldn't pull him.

Chameleon took the other end of the rope down to
the river, and disguised himself as a branch.
　　And when Crocodile came slithering along,
Chameleon threw the rope round his neck, calling:
　　"Now that I have you on a rope I shall pull you along!
Just wait until I pull."

　　"I'll wait," laughed Crocodile.

And Chameleon walked back to the middle of the
rope where he could just see Crocodile to the right.
And he could just see Leopard to the left.
And Chameleon became the same color as a leaf
so they could not see him, and yelled, "Pull!"

Leopard pulled first, and Crocodile came whizzing
and splashing backwards through the mud,
his little legs whirring around and around.

Then Crocodile pulled hard, and Leopard was dragged through a nest of biting ants.

Then Leopard pulled ... then Crocodile ...
then Leopard.
   Until both animals were exhausted
from being dragged all over the forest.

"I am sorry, Mr Chameleon, I will never bother you again, I promise!" they each called. "Please let me go."

And when they sat down panting, Chameleon came and cut them free.

And to this day, the Crocodile and the Leopard
do not bother the Chameleon. They leave him alone.
For brains are often better than strength or size.

And Chameleon can go as slow as he likes.
But just in case the animals find out about
the trick he played, he changes color and hides
when he hears them coming.

That is the end.